Paul Bunyan

In the days of the wild north country, everything was bigger. Rivers were wider and mountains were higher and men were bigger, too. The biggest man of all was Paul Bunyan. He was so big that he could fell ten giant trees with one sharp swoop of his ax. One day Paul found a baby ox. Paul named him Babe and together they roamed the land.

This is an easy-to-read story about the time when our country was very young and very tall.

A SEE AND READ
Beginning to Read Story Book

PAUL
BUNYAN

By Maxine W. Kumin

Illustrated by Dirk Gringhuis

G. P. Putnam's Sons   New York

For Danny

Published simultaneously in the Dominion of
Canada by Longmans Canada Limited, Toronto
Library of Congress Catalog Card Number: 66-10455
PRINTED IN THE UNITED STATES OF AMERICA
07209

PAUL BUNYAN

In the days of Paul Bunyan, the
north country was a wild place.
The woods were full of tall trees.
The rivers were young and fast
moving. The winters were colder,
the snow was deeper then. Men
were bigger, too. And the biggest
of all was Paul Bunyan.

Paul was the biggest baby in all of Maine. When he rolled over in his sleep, four miles of trees fell down. Men cut up the broken trees and made a cradle for Paul. They pulled it out to sea way up north. Then they put the big baby in it.

Every time Paul moved, the cradle rocked. Every time the cradle rocked, it made a wave higher than the treetops. The tide climbed and climbed. Waves washed into houses all along the coast of Canada.

"Do something!" the people cried.

His father and mother hurried to pull Paul back to dry land. They brought him to the edge of Nova Scotia. But when Paul got out of his cradle, another big wall of water started moving. This time the tide was forty feet high. The tide is still coming in up there in the Bay of Fundy, between Nova Scotia and New Brunswick.

Thanks to Paul, the Bay of Fundy
has the biggest tides in the world.

Paul grew up, foot by foot. At last he was old enough to go to school. But he was much too big to fit into the schoolroom. He could not read from books because the ABC's were too small. His teacher made a great A on the face of a straight hill. It took him four days to wash it off. Next, it took him a week to write a B. The poor teacher never got to C.

"I can't do it, Paul," he said. "My legs are too tired from climbing up and down this hill."

Paul was sad that he never learned to read and write. But he did know A from B.

As soon as he was old enough to leave home, Paul headed west. He wanted to be a logger. In four steps he walked up into the blue mountains of Ontario. It was night-time there. Paul picked up his heavy ax and banged it against the dark. A crack opened along the east. He hit the sky again, harder. Stars fell down and some blue sky peeped through. The sun found its

way through the broken place. Paul
jumped down from the mountain in
one jump. From then on he was
Day Breaker for all the loggers in
the woods.

Paul was a great logger himself. He cut through the biggest trees as if they were butter. He kept the cutting side of his ax as bright as silver. He could swish through ten trees at a time with one cut. They all fell over in a straight line, too.

One thing gave Paul a lot of trouble out in the woods. He never knew what time it was. No watch in America was big enough for Paul to use.

"I know what we can do," said his friend, Johnny Inkslinger. "They are taking down an old city hall out west. There is a big clock on top of the building. Let's buy it as a surprise for Paul."

Johnny Inkslinger and some of the loggers went to the city. They got the big clock from the city hall. They made it into a fine watch. It was big enough for Paul to use as a pocket watch. The minute hand was six feet long. The face was as wide and as round as a duck pond.

Paul's clock-watch rang four times
every hour. It made such a loud
noise that all the deer in the woods
ran away. The wheel on Paul's
watch was hard to wind. The men
used an engine to turn the wheel.
But they only had to wind it on
the Fourth of July and on
Christmas Day.

Soon Paul had his own loggers'
camp. It was the best camp in the
north woods. The cook worked very
hard with so many men to feed.
But the loggers were cross every
morning. They did not want to
wake up when Paul broke the day.

"We're hungry," they said. "We want pancakes for breakfast."

The poor cook could not make pancakes fast enough in one small pan.

"I'll fix that," said Paul. He went to his friends the farmers and asked them for their old plows. The front end of a walking plow looks something like a shovel. Paul hammered a lot of plow shovels together. It took more plow shovels than you could count to make that griddle. When it was done, Paul rolled the griddle back to camp like a wheel.

How wide was it? Well, the loggers
took turns skating across it with
bacon on their shoes. After the
bacon cooked down a little, the
griddle was ready for pancakes.
From then on, the loggers were
happy to wake up. It was hot
bacon and pancakes, hot pancakes
and bacon every cold morning. And
it was very cold in the north woods
in the morning.

But the winter of the blue snow
was the coldest winter of all. It
was so cold that the ponds froze all
the way to the bottom. The loggers
had to take the ice out to warm
up the fish. In some places, the ice
froze so fast that it stayed hot. It
was too hot to cut up for water!

When people talked, their words froze in the air. It was spring before you could tell what they had been saying. No one needed to talk all summer, there were so many words left over.

Timber

And then the snow came down
all blue. There were blue snow-
banks ten feet tall. When the cows
had some of that blue snow-water,
they gave blue milk.

Johnny Inkslinger worked in Paul's
camp. Every week he counted the
money each logger had earned. But
Johnny could not add in his head,
and he did not have a pen. He
used to write on paper with a piece
of burned wood. His 4's and 7's
and 9's all ran together. Then came
the blue snow. Johnny Inkslinger
caught some and let it warm up.
He made a hole in a stick from
the top to the bottom. The hole at
the bottom was very small.

Then he filled the stick with blue snow-water. That was the first pen. Now Johnny could make his 4's and 7's and 9's come out right.

Paul was out looking for his lost dog in the blue snow. He walked as far as the North Pole on his snowshoes. The dog found his way home all by himself. At last Paul came back to camp, too. But he was not alone. He was carrying a great big bright blue baby ox!

The baby ox was hungry. But no one fed him. The men were all busy with a logjam in the river. Logs were crowded every which way, from bank to bank. When the ox mooed, the building shook. Logs in the logjam fell into line. When he mooed again, the logs started to move.

Paul named his blue ox Babe. At
first he did not know what to feed
Babe. Then he remembered something good. Moose moss! Moose
moss would be just right for Babe.
Paul hurried to the mountain where
the moose moss grew. He picked
some and cooked it in a big pot.
Babe was so delighted with his
moose moss dinner that he ate the
pot, too.

The baby ox grew straight and
strong in Paul's camp. He was
much bigger than the biggest
moose. How big did Babe grow to
be? Well, a pet crow used to stand
on one of Babe's horns. One day
the crow set out to fly across to
Babe's other horn. It took that crow
all winter to fly across Babe's head.
It was spring before he reached the
other horn.

No one ever knew where Babe
had really come from. But he be-
came Paul's best friend and helper.
Babe loved to go logging. Each
morning he galloped off into the
forest. He raced the loggers over
rocks and stones to the best trees.

Paul's loggers went to work cutting down the trees. Then Babe pulled them to the river as if they were tiny sticks. The fat logs splashed into the river. The loggers pushed them along with big poles. At last the logs came to the sawmill. All day long at the sawmill, buzz saws cut up the logs. Now there was enough wood to make homes all over America.

Babe the blue ox was big enough and jolly enough for anything. He and Paul always worked together. They pulled all the hooks and bumps and turns out of the logging roads. They stood at each end of turning rivers and pulled them out straight.

The straight rivers were shorter than the roundabout ones they started with. What could Paul do with the leftover pieces?

"Someone can use these," said Paul. So he rolled them up for Babe to carry. Then he rolled them out again in dry places that needed rivers. Paul made most of the rivers out west that way.

One day Paul and Babe got a
letter from the farmers in Kansas.
The letter asked for help. At that
time, Kansas was full of rolling
mountains. There was very little
room to grow anything. Paul got a
big shovel for Babe to pull. In two
days they had shoveled Kansas
down into bottomland. Now the
farmers could plant fields of corn.
Paul and Babe used the leftover
dirt to make the Rocky Mountains.

The Rocky Mountains were a good thing for the farmers. They kept the cold winds from whipping through the cornfields. Now the corn did not blow out of the ground in the Middle West.

At about this time, there was a mountain growing upside down in the Dakotas. The trees on it grew upside down, too. The tip of the mountain grew into the ground. The loggers could not cut through upside-down trees. The trees would fall down on them. They could not stand on their heads all day to work. What could they do?

"That's easy," said Paul. He shot the trees down with his shotgun. Babe pulled them to the river. The hard work made Babe very hungry. He started to eat the tip of the mountain. He was so hungry that he ate right through the rock. Now there was nothing holding up the mountain. It fell down into lots of little pieces. The little pieces made the Black Hills of the Dakotas.

In the days of Paul Bunyan, our
country was still a wild place. The
woods were full of tall trees.
America was full of tall stories.
Now that their work is done, Paul
and Babe are resting. Maybe we
will need them again someday.
Maybe someday Paul and Babe will
move some more mountains and
make some more rivers. Who
knows? Maybe they will fix up the
moon for people to live on.

Key Words

bacon	plow
cradle	pole
froze	sawmill
griddle	shotgun
hall	tide
logger	wind
moose	winding
moss	

Other SEE AND READ
Beginning to Read Biographies

The Author

MAXINE W. KUMIN is a most imaginative author of books for younger children. Her recent work, *The Beach Before Breakfast*, was nominated for a Caldecott Medal. The author writes both prose and poetry, as evidenced by *Speedy Digs Downside Up, No One Writes a Letter to the Snail*, and *Eggs of Things*. Mrs. Kumin, her husband and three children live in Newton Highlands, Massachusetts.

The Artist

DIRK GRINGHUIS has been a lifelong fan of Paul Bunyan. He has used him in the theme for a mural on Michigan folklore, and is presently a producer-teacher of a television series on Michigan history with the accent on logging. Mr. Gringhuis has also done two books on the history of lumbering as well as a number of juvenile books including the recent *Daniel Boone*.